MAMA SHAMSI
at the BAZAAR

by **MOJDEH HASSANI** and **SAMIRA IRAVANI**

illustrated by **MAYA FIDAWI**

Dial Books for Young Readers

Samira and her grandmother live in a busy city called Tehran. Today, Mama Shamsi is walking with her zanbil to the big bazaar in the middle of the city to buy groceries.

Samira is going with her grandmother for the very first time.

"Mama Shams, Mama Shams!
Will the bazaar be loud?
How big will it be?
Will I get lost in the crowd?"

"Na, na, na."

She puts on her chador.
"You'll stay right by me while
we walk through the stores."

"Mama Shams, Mama Shams!
Let me ride on your back,
curled in your chador,
so warm and so black."

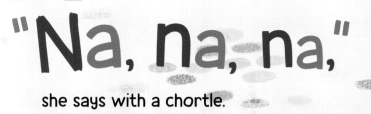

"Na, na, na,"

she says with a chortle.
"Our neighbors will think that I am a turtle!"

"Mama Shams, Mama Shams!
Let's get in a line,
under your chador,
you in front, me behind!"

"Na, na, na,

I'll look like a fool
with four legs below me just like a mule!"

"Mama Shams, Mama Shams!
I think I could squeeze
up front by your belly!
Will you let me, please?"

"Na, na, na,

You know what they'll do?
They'll see my big bump and say:
Look! Kangaroo!"

One last time, Samira tries:

"Mama Shams, Mama Shams!
Let me up all the way!
With your chador on my head
I won't go astray."

"Na, na, na,"

Shamsi says with a laugh.

"The merchants will say that I'm a giraffe!"

They finally reach the street before the bazaar. If Mama Shamsi won't let her under the chador, what will Samira do when it gets loud and crowded? She thinks hard and asks:

"Then Mama Shams,
how will I know
where you are in the shops
and which way to go?"

Mama Shamsi looks at her little helper.

"You'll use your eyes and your ears,
even your nose too,
to explore this world
and learn what's around you!"

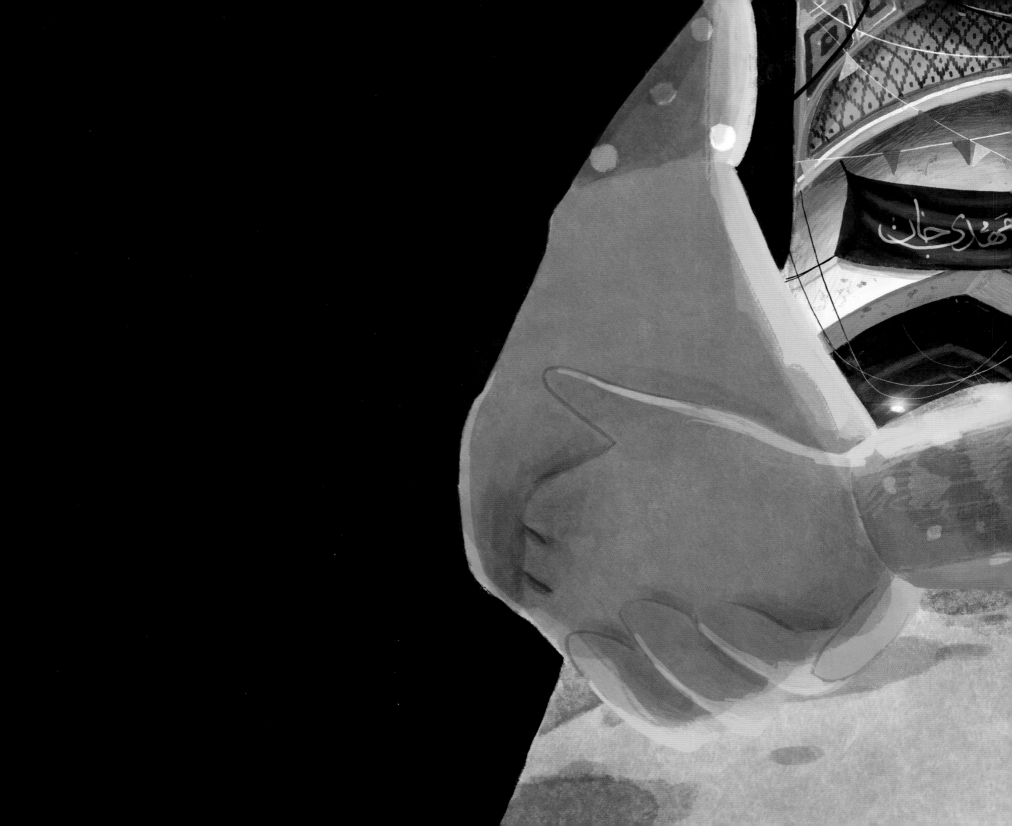

"And hold my hand, azizam,"
she says as they cross.

"With Grandmother beside you,
you'll never be lost."

To my maman, who has been my loving teacher and light, and to my girls,
Samira and Laila, who are my life. —Mojdeh Hassani

To maman, who inspired my love of books.
And to Mama Shamsi, who inspired us all. —Samira Iravani

My dedication goes to my dear country Lebanon, and my beloved city Beirut, the ever suffering little
place that's never ceased seeking life and resilience even during its worst days. And also to my children,
Karim and Salma, the two rays of light that keep me going, and to my mom and dad. —Maya Fidawi

Dial Books for Young Readers
An imprint of Penguin Random House LLC, New York

First published in the United States of America by Dial Books for Young Readers,
an imprint of Penguin Random House LLC, 2022

Text copyright © 2022 by Mojdeh Hassani and Samira Iravani • Illustrations copyright © 2022 by Maya Fidawi Zihri

Visit us online at penguinrandomhouse.com.

Library of Congress Cataloging-in-Publication Data is available.

Manufactured in China
ISBN 9780593110614
TOPL

1 3 5 7 9 10 8 6 4 2

Design by Mina Chung and Lily Malcom • Text set in Caffe Lungo
The publisher does not have any control over and does not assume any responsibility for author or third-party websites or their content.

The artwork of this book was created digitally, using procreate app on iPad Pro.

A Note from the Authors

MOJDEH: While the story you've just read is fiction, the people, places, and things in this book are rooted in my very real childhood growing up in Tehran in the 1960s and '70s. Presiding over all was the real Mama Shamsi, my maternal grandmother, whose charisma and wisdom held sway over her entire family. Despite the many offerings of my historic and metropolitan home city, my favorite place to play was always under Mama Shamsi's black chador. It was a warm and tender space that captivated my imagination just like a stage-curtain fabric that I could fan open and shut to create marvelous imaginary scenes!

SAMIRA: And while the Samira in this tale enjoys the weekly walk to the bazaar, living in the U.S. meant I never got that special privilege. I grew up with my mother's stories of her life in Iran, doing my best to imagine what it was like. The only thing I *didn't* have to dream up was undoubtedly the best part: playing in my grandmother's chador. I too cherish my memories of sneaking under that perfumed cloth, pretending to be a grown-up, a magical queen, or any of the silly critters you see in our story.

Our wish in writing this book is to add to the growing list of stories for children that demystify this veil (that is too often used as a symbol of hate) and instead present a different view of it as the safe and comforting space we always knew it to be.

Other real things our readers may notice in this book are: a *zanbil* (carried by Samira), which is a large woven basket often used to carry groceries; a *Shahr-e-Farang* (p. 15, 35), a gold apparatus with a small viewing port that revealed moving images, which children could watch for a small fee; a *joob* (p. 23), the open canals that line the roads in Tehran to carry rainwater away; food vendors selling bread (p.23), grilled corn (p. 34), and Mojdeh's favorite, steamed beets (p. 35), whose sweet red juice was the perfect thing to warm you up in winter; and finally, the Tajrish Bazaar (p. 27, 32–35), a thriving market that stands to this day, selling everything you could possibly dream of, from spices to jewels.